AF409370

I LOVE YOU MORE

CORNELIA AMIRI

I LOVE YOU MORE

A mother's love never fails...it always prevails.

On the verge of turning sixty, Garland recalls memories and moments of her life's journey from an abusive childhood to a bad marriage to the ups and downs of a single mom. She is rewarded with a magical mother's day with her son, daughter in law, and granddaughter. Her moving story is sure to touch your heart.

CHAPTER 1

Texas 2016

She smiled at the crayon drawing held by magnets on the refrigerator door. Judson drew it for her, for Mother's Day, when he was six. Garland opened the refrigerator door, took out the jug of sweet tea and poured herself a glass.

Today was Mother's day and Judson was on his way to pick her up and take her out. She took her glass of tea and sat on the sofa. He didn't live with her anymore. Her baby was 34 now and he'd moved out years ago.

She sipped her drink and petted her cat as she gazed at the framed photographs on top of her entertainment center of Judson and his wife and his daughter. Their smiling faces. She leaned back on the sofa.

The first time she met him face to face Garland was strapped down to an operating table because she'd just had a C-section. When the doctor told her it was a boy, she said, "Judson." He wasn't just a boy he was Judson.

The pediatrician there at the birth brought him to her, holding him up beside her head. She turned her neck and kissed his forehead. Every vein in her body had sung with joy. Happiness at a level that couldn't even be described had flowed through her. There never was before and had never been since, a happier moment in Garland's life.

And Judson had grown into a wonderful man.

Garland looked at her huge, gray and black striped cat and said to him, "Judson worked his way up from a stocker to a regional position; making enough to support his wife and child."

Garland had felt terrible that she hadn't been able to earn enough to send Judson to college, but that hadn't stopped her baby.

"You know Amber," Garland said to her cat, Severus.

Judson had met Amber, his wife, at the grocery store they worked at when she was a bakery manager and he was a grocery manager.

"She's Judson's wife. You know Judson."

Severus meowed in response.

"Yes, you know Judson. He's like your brother. He lived here when you were a kitten."

His wife was wonderful. Garland knew if anything happened to her, Amber would take care of her baby and her granddaughter. Garland had a granddaughter now. She was ten, which seemed impossible. It seemed like she was just a small baby yesterday.

"Judson and Amber are coming here today, and Sydney too. So I'll be gone for a little bit. It's Mother's Day." She petted Severus as he blinked his huge jade-toned eyes at her.

Amber, his wife, was like a daughter to her. Not only that, Amber's family had accepted Garland as family from day one. Every Thanksgiving and Christmas she was invited to their house along with Judson, Amber, and Sydney.

She glanced at the time on her cell phone, which was on the coffee table. He'd be here soon.

Garland's childhood had been a pack of lies. The family she'd been born into didn't fit the definition of what anyone thought of as a family. Born in the fifties, when child abuse was considered to not exist, there had been no one to help her. She'd spent her whole childhood and young adult years with people that didn't want the best for her. They wanted to hurt her, when her father would beat her he told her he wanted to kill her, he wanted her to die. There wasn't anything she could do about that.

But when Judson created his family he in turn gave her additional family members as well. Once again her son had come through for her in ways she couldn't imagine

"Punkin will be here soon," she said to Severus as he purred, siting on her lap.

Every Mother's Day, just like today, Judson visited her and took her out to eat with him, Sydney, and Amber.

Her phone rang, she grabbed it. The words, my son, identified the caller. She'd programmed that in because Siri couldn't understand the name Judson. Garland pushed the accept call dot.

"Hey Mom, Sydney and I are coming up."

She opened the door and they stood in front of her. Sydney rushed past Garland, into the apartment, went straight to Severus, bent down and started petting him.

"Hi mom." Judson pulled Garland into his arms, in a bracing hug.

"Nana!" Sydney left the cat, ran to Garland and gave her a big hug.

Garland noticed that Severus turned and sauntered

away, heading for the bedroom. Too many humans in here for his taste and it was time for another nap.

Judson's face was as bright as the sun due to his big smile as he handed Garland a bouquet of spring flowers. "Happy Mother's Day."

"Thank you, punkin. They're beautiful." The fresh scents of tulips, narcissi and daffodils danced in the air.

Garland took the flowers into the kitchen where she placed them in a vase full of water on her small round table.

Sydney plopped down onto the sofa to watch the program Garland had been looking at, an old rerun of a Lawrence Welk Mother's Day episode with Lynn Anderson singing Mother May I with her mother.

"What is this show?" Sydney asked. "Why are they dressed a like?"

"It's an old show, I think that episode was from the 60's but it's about Mother's Day. They're mother and daughter so they dressed to sing together on the show."

"I've never seen it before," Sydney said. "They're dressed like old days."

"Like the 60's because that's when this show was filmed. It's a rerun."

"It's that old?"

"Yes, an antique, right?" Garland laughed.

"Did you dress like that?" Sydney asked.

"Not exactly, in the 60's I was a kid and also a tween like you are now. I did have a yellow dress with Swiss dots like that and ruffles but it didn't have a full skirt. It had a straight shape like a shirtdress. But when I was in first through third grade I wore all these little A-line dresses and I always wore a slip with ruffles under them. And we wore something called undershirts that people seem to call wife beaters now. And we couldn't wear pants to school, only dresses until Jr. High, you call it middle school, then we could wear pantsuits."

"Do you still wear those dresses?"

"No, silly, I can't fit into anything I wore back then."

Judson joined them on the sofa. "I looked up some places that are having special Mother's Day brunches."

"Sounds great. I like poached eggs."

"'I think the nearest one, which has a five-star rating, is in Bellaire, so that's real close."

"Yes, let's go."

Garland followed her son and granddaughter to the car.

As he held the door for her, he said, "Amber had to work, she's sorry she couldn't make it."

She sat in the front seat as Sydney plopped down in the back.

"No that's fine, yall both work so hard. How is she?"

"She's great." Judson started the car. "Everything is great. How is everything with you?"

"Good. I'm writing. Still trying to sell more books, trying to find ways to promote them better."

"I'm so proud of you, Mom, all the books you've written."

"I'm proud of you. So proud." Even in that moment, tears of joy threatened to spill out again. Just being with Judson made Garland happy.

TEXAS 1982

She woke, changed Judson's diaper and put him in his walker. Then she threw on a t-shirt and jeans and headed into the kitchen.

Her husband stood by the counter, drinking a cup of

coffee. "I'm going to take a walk and get a newspaper from the little store," he said.

"Okay. You're not going to take the car?"

"No. I need to walk."

Samuel left and Garland let out a sigh of relief. This was her chance to leave with the baby. She couldn't help but think how ironic it was that today was Mother's Day.

Her mind flashed back to earlier that week, when she got home from work, and stepped inside her apartment, her husband had smacked her in the face.

She recalled he'd yelled, "Where have you been?"

She'd still been reeling, trying to get her bearings. He'd never hit her before. She didn't' know what was going on. "I had to work overtime, I called and told you. What's wrong?"

"The baby was crying for you and you weren't here. You were at work with your boss."

"Not my boss, a co-worker. The boss went home at the same time he always does."

He slapped her again and again. Finally, he stopped and walked away into the family room. She started to cry but pulled herself together. Judson needed her. She ran to Judson's room. He stood in his crib, dressed in a diaper and a tiny green t-shirt, crying. He, reached his arms out to her.

She picked him up. "It's okay. Mama's here."

His cry sounded like a hunger cry. In her arms, he'd stopped crying and she carried him to the kitchen. It had confused her because Samuel should have fed him by then, it was 8 pm.

She remembered sitting Judson in his high chair. Samuel was sitting on the sofa watching TV but he didn't say anything to her and she sure didn't speak to him.

She'd grabbed two jars of baby food, chicken sticks and diced peaches, opened them and put them on Judson's plate, then she had snatched his toddler spoon and fork from the drawer. She'd set all that on his high chair tray, pulled up a chair in front of him and sat.

He'd grabbed a chicken stick with his chubby fingers, held it to his mouth and gobbled it down. And he'd devoured the peaches just as fast. It seemed like his father hadn't fed him.

As Judson ate she asked Samuel, "Did you feed the baby?"

"This baby did nothing but cry. I couldn't feed him. I couldn't do anything and it's all your fault. You were with your boss instead of with your baby like a good mother."

She'd glanced at Judson as he was finishing up his chicken fingers. Then she filled his sippy cup with milk. She had handed it to Judson and he'd quickly drunk it. He'd seemed full, so she'd lifted him out of the highchair, but when she'd tried to set him down on the floor so he could walk, he'd cried, making it clear he wanted her to hold him. She'd carried him to the bedroom and they both fell asleep in her bed.

The next day at work she'd used her lunch break making phone calls. Houston had several shelters for battered women but they were all filled up, except for one.

On Saturday, she had tried to leave with Judson in hand, but her husband had told her she could go but she couldn't take the baby. She'd left just to drive to the shelter to get all the information she'd needed and to make sure they had a place for her, then she came back home.

That was yesterday. Garland pulled herself from her reflections and took a deep breath. She lifted Judson out of his walker, grabbed her purse and walked out the front door. Samuel could come back at any moment. She had to figure this out. This could be her one and only chance to get out with Judson. As she walked through the apartment complex to the parking lot she saw a woman walking up an outside staircase.

She had to do this. She waked toward her briskly with Judson in her arms. "Hello. We haven't met, I live in apartment 40. I have to ask you something. You can say no if you want but I have to ask."

"I don't think so," she said as she continued up the stairs. She wore a blue print blouse and white jeans, her afro was short but her earrings were long.

Judson waved his tiny chubby hand at the retreating woman.

Garland walked up to the staircase. "I'm leaving my husband, he's been hitting me. He said I could go but I can't take the baby. He's getting a newspaper. He'll be back any moment."

The lady's expression was indifferent, even bothered, until the last sentence then it changed to one of concern. She headed back down the stairs. "Do you want me to call the police?"

"No, I don't think that will help. We're married, so in Texas Judson is a hundred percent my son and a hundred percent my husband's son. I have to get away and file for divorce to have a chance of stopping him from taking my baby away."

"When will you come back?" Her expression looked doubtful and her brow furrowed.

"Right away. As soon as I get my suitcase and even if my husband returns, I'll be right back. I have a shelter l lined up, where we're going." She held her breath, waiting for the woman's answer, she expected her to say no.

The lady reached her arms out and took the baby. "I'm

Rena. I live in 18, right up there." She pointed to the door upstairs.

Garland repeated 18 again and again in her mind. "This is Judson and I'm Garland, I live in 40."

"How can I reach you if anything happens?" Rena asked as she held Judson close against her.

"Well, I can give you my phone number but my husband will answer. I'll also give you the number for the shelter." She dug into her purse, pulled out some old receipt and a pen then jotted the numbers on the back of it. She handed it to Rena.

"Since we don't know each other, can I see your driver's license?" Her friendly, personable expression changed to a serious, aloof one again. "I would just feel better."

"Sure." Garland showed Rena her driver's license and she seemed satisfied. "I'll take good care of him until you get back."

Garland thanked her. She didn't have much time but she felt she had to get some information since she was handing her baby over to a stranger. Due to the bad circumstances it seemed like a good idea and she had no other alternative, but still. "Can you give me your phone number and last name?"

Rena told her and she jotted it down on the back of another receipt, then stuffed it in her purse.

She patted Judson on the head. "Mama will be right back."

She ran to her apartment to get her stuff out as quick as she could. She flew inside and called out, "Samuel."

There was no answer, he wasn't back yet. She rushed into her bedroom, yanked the closet door open, grabbed the suitcase and swung it onto the bed. She unlatched it and threw in diapers, Judson's clothes and her clothes as rapidly as she could. She shut it and grabbing the handle, she ran to the front door and wrenched it open.

Samuel stood there.

She cringed. Why did he come in the front door instead of the back? Did he know?

"Going somewhere?" He blocked the way out with his body, much larger than her 5"3" 120 lb build.

He had a gleam to his eye that made her feel like he thought they were playing a game and he'd won.

"I'm leaving."

"You have nowhere to go."

"I do have somewhere to go."

"Where?"

"That's my business. But you said I could go and I am."

"So you are leaving your baby just like that?" He put both hands on his hips and peered down at her with a sneer on his face.

"Yes, now." She steeled her courage and confidence and tried to push past him.

He grabbed the suitcase from her. "What's in here?"

"My clothes." She was afraid he'd open it and see Judson's things. Then he'd know. Her muscles stiffened and a jittery sensation engulfed her.

"You can't take anything out of this house." He shoved past her inside the apartment and the force of that pushed her outside where he'd stood a moment before. That was good.

"Why won't you let me take my clothes? That's all that's in there."

He leaned his head down to her and yelled loudly.

"You want to leave. Go. You are the only thing I don't want. Everything else has to stay."

"Fine. It's just clothes." She swallowed hard and looked him in the eyes. "Good bye, Samuel."

Little did he know, she had the important treasure out of the house already, Judson. She turned and walked away as calmly as she could. She heard the door slam and slowly turned her head to make sure he was inside. He was. She had to hurry, soon he'd find out the baby was gone. She ran upstairs to Rena's apartment and knocked on the door.

Rena opened it. "You're back already. What's up? Where's your suitcase?"

"He came back and he wouldn't let me take the suitcase."

Rena's eyes widened.

Garland quickly added, "But it's okay. I'll buy what I need."

"What about Judson?"

"He doesn't know the baby's gone yet. That's why I have to leave now."

"Well, I'm glad I could help. You take care."

Garland took her baby in her arms, he was calm and happy, he had no idea they were running away. She thanked Rena one last time and rushed down the stairs and out the gate to the garage. She grabbed her key from her purse, unlocked the car and fastened Judson into his car seat.

The car belonged to her before she married and was in her name only so Samuel couldn't say she stole it or anything. She jumped into the driver seat and took off toward the shelter, clear on the other side of town.

She'd made it. She parked at the shelter and walked inside to the office. The lady working there was the same one who she'd spoken to when she'd come yesterday.

"Hi, Mrs. Jones, you can still take me and my baby right?"

"Call me Doretha, and yes we can. Is this him?" The lady in the blue dress walked up to them and smiled brightly at Judson. "Such a cute baby."

"Thank you." Garland smiled brightly. Judson wouldn't be around violence. She'd gotten him away from that. He'd be fine now.

"Have a seat." Doretha pointed to an armchair in front of the desk.

Garland eased down into it, holding Judson. She initialled and signed some papers where the lady indicated.

"Here are the rules." Doretha handed her a list of standard items. "Now everyone has chores except those that work, they don't have to do daily chores."

"I work at an insurance company. I process checks—clerical work."

"You won't have assigned chores then. Do you have someone to watch him while you work?"

"No, my husband wasn't working so he took care of him. I guess I'll have to find a nursery close by."

"You won't have to do that. We have women here that baby sit the children of the working mothers. I think they charge $10.00 a day."

"That's great. Yes, I'll do that."

"Do you have your suitcase in the car?"

"No, my husband wouldn't let me take anything out of the house."

"But you got him out like you said you would." Doretha pointed to Judson still in Garland's arms.

"I did."

"You didn't tell him where you are?

"No!" Garland shook her head. "I didn't say anything to him about where I was going. Which reminds me, is there a pay phone the residents can use. I need to call work tomorrow to get the day off and call around to find a lawyer. I want to file divorce right away. My husband's from another country and I want to make sure he doesn't find a way to get Judson and leave the U. S. with him."

She picked up the phone on her desk. "Right here. You can use it anytime you want for work or things you need to do. We have a pay phone for talking to your friends and that kind of thing." Doretha stood. "Here let me show you around."

Garland set Judson down and took his hand in hers as they followed the lady.

"This is the cafeteria and we have super here tonight at 6 pm. We're having a special ham dinner for Mother's Day."

"Oh, that's nice."

Doretha led them to the next room.

"This is the family area. We have a TV in here you can watch and that's the payphone there."

Garland noticed the women and children watching TV and talking to each other. She spotted a chest of toys against the wall. It seemed a good place to stay until she could get an apartment on her own.

She and Judson followed Doretha down the hall to the bedrooms.

She entered one with two twin beds. A young girl with blonde hair sat on one and a child about Judson's age played on the floor.

"This is Janelle and her baby." Doretha smiled at Janelle. "This is Garland and her son."

The girl smiled and pointed to her boy. "This is Sean."

Judson sat on the floor with him.

"Hello." Garland walked up to Janelle. "Nice to meet you."

"Same here. I picked out this bed for Sean and me, if that's okay?"

"Sure." She sat down on the twin bed that would be hers and Judson's.

Doretha said, "Well I'll leave you to get settled. If you need anything, just let me know."

Janelle flashed a bright smile. "Happy Mother's Day, Garland!"

She felt like sunshine streamed through her at those words. It was a happy Mother's Day. She and Judson were safe and had a new start.

She smiled at her new roommate. "Happy Mother's Day to you too."

CHAPTER 2

Texas 2016

Garland walked with her son and granddaughter into the large restaurant full of mothers crowded around tables with their families.

The hostess greeted them, "Happy Mother's Day." She handed Garland a complimentary pink carnation.

"Thank you." Garland held it out to Sydney.

Sydney took a whiff and glanced at Judson. "There's no smell."

"Florists bred out the fragrance so the flowers would last longer. It's a shame, I love to smell flowers." Garland let out a long sigh.

"Did the ones I gave you smell?" Judson asked.

"I think they did. They were so pretty, thank you, Punkin."

Judson gave the hostess the name on the reservation and she led them to a table where Garland was overcome with shock. She gasped from the thrilling surprise.

Amber was at the table with a bright smile on her face

that made her eyes shine. She'd waited for them, holding two bouquets of yellow balloons. Happy Mother's Day was written on each balloon.

"Surprise," Judson called out to her.

Amber jumped to her feet and drew Garland into her arms for a big hug.

"I thought you had to work." Garland was still shocked form the wonderful surprise.

"Happy Mother's Day! This was all Judson's idea for me and for you. He wanted to surprise you." Amber sat back down.

Garland took a seat, as did Judson and Sydney.

Sydney yelled out, "Happy Mother's Day, Mom and Nana."

"Thank you." Amber hugged Sydney and gave her a kiss.

Garland pulled her granddaughter into her arms for a big hug. "Thank you all so much. Happy Mother's Day to you, Amber."

"Happy Mother's Day, babe." Judson leaned over to his wife and kissed her on the mouth. Then he leaned over to Garland. "Happy Mother's Day." And he kissed her on the cheek.

"This is the best Mother's Day I've ever had." Garland wiped a tear of joy from the corner of her eye.

The waitress bought the grownups mimosas and gave Sidney a sprite.

Amber smiled. "I ordered the drinks for us."

Judson lifted his champagne flute. "To my wife and my mom, the two best mothers anyone has ever had." He clinked his glass with Amber's and then with Garland's.

Amber had gotten menus for everyone so Garland looked hers over.

A thin, blonde waiter came and Judson's mouth dropped open. "What? No way! I didn't know you worked here."

"Yeah, I do. It's a good job." The waiter smiled.

Judson glanced at Garland. "Mom, you remember David."

She remembered Judson's friend, but she didn't know why he mentioned him now. "Yes."

He looked at the waiter and she looked at him also. "David? I didn't recognize you." She laughed. He looked so different. The last time she'd seen David he was in high school along with Judson. He looked so different. Older, too old for his age, the same as Judson.

"It's good to see you," David said to her.

"This is my wife, Amber and my daughter, Sydney."

David shook their hands. Then he nodded at Garland. "Are you ready to order?"

"Yes." He was at work and they were taking up his time. The place was crowded. She put in her order. "Poached eggs." She loved the taste of them, loved the way the sunny yolk bled out against the white of the egg and onto the plate.

Everyone else ordered including Sydney who had to go gluten-free due to her allergy.

When David left, Garland turned to Judson. "He was the cutest of your friends and now he looks so different. He looks wrinkled but he's much too young for that.

"Is he the one you told me about?" Amber glanced at Judson.

"Yes," He answered his wife and turned to Garland. "David has had a hard time. He got on drugs. He had hallucinations so bad his mother had to call the police because he started choking her. He didn't know who she was."

"What?" David had always been shy and sweet.

"It was drugs," Judson whispered as he leaned closer to Garland. "I didn't know he worked here. The last time I talked to him, he was having a hard time finding a job."

"Oh no." Garland shook her head, thinking about Judson's friends from High School. One had recently lost his fingers from a factory accident. One worked as an artist but he couldn't keep a job for more than a few months and was divorced with a child. "Of all your high school friends, you're doing the best."

"I am." Judson took a sip of his mimosa.

"I don't want to let some of Judson's old friends into the house," Amber said.

"You've done so well Judson." Garland glanced at Amber. "You too. I am so proud of both of you."

David soon returned with their food and Garland took a bite of her poached egg.

She put her fork down and said, "Thank you for this Mother's Day brunch. It's is a great brunch with the best company." She took in a deep breath and just took a moment to enjoy the company of her loving family. She was so choked up with happiness she could barely drink her Mimosa.

TEXAS 1987

Garland, in her best dress, a white one with big black polka dots and wide sleeves, and wearing her black business pumps, walked into the church with the other parents for the special evening performance for Mother's Day. She sat on a pew near the front where she'd have a good view. Energy swirled inside her, she was bursting with excitement, she could hardly wait for the six-year-old Sunday school class to perform— Judson's class.

Mrs. Barnes came out short yet poufy hairstyle. "Next, is our six-year-old Sunbeams class. Each child will be holding an original drawing they did of their mother and what their mother means to them. Then the class will sing a special Mother's Day song.

The children walked onto the stage, each holding their picture proudly. Garland felt a fluttery warmth in her chest. She sat up straight and fixed her gaze and her smile on Judson. He held up a picture of a stick figure lady with red hair and a big smile and a stick figure boy, stood next to her. A huge yellow sun shone above their heads. It was the most beautiful work of art she'd ever seen. A picture of her family: her and Judson.

Judson softly and slowly sang to the tune of You Are My Sunshine, "You make me happy, when I am sad."

Half way through the song Judson stopped and looked directly at her with a lost expression. She nodded to him as she flashed a huge smile of encouragement.

He sang louder than ever, "I want to tell you, I really love you." Garland clapped as hard and as loud as she could.

Mrs. Barnes stepped up to each child, one by one, bending down so she was eye level with them. She asked them who their parents were, and then they went to sit with their family.

Mrs. Barnes stepped up to Judson and bent down to him. "Who are your mother and father." With a huge smile on his face, he said, "My mother and father is Garland." He pointed to her, proudly.

Garland had to blink back the tears. Judson ran down

from the stage holding his picture and handed it to her, then took his place at her side in the pew.

It was the second happiest moment in her life. She was Judson's mother and father and he was so proud... as proud as she was.

CHAPTER 3

Texas 2016

Garland lifted her glass and took a swallow of the last of her Mimosa.

Judson and Amber glanced at each other then they both set their gaze on her. Both flashed bright grins.

"We have another surprise for you," Judson said.

"We're going to the movies," Sydney piped up.

"Would you like to come with us?" Judson took a final sip of his coffee. "That movie Mothers and Daughters is playing. I thought you'd really like that."

"I've been wanting to see it. Today's the perfect day," Amber remarked, as she wiped the crumbs up in front of Sydney.

"Have you seen it yet, Mom?" Judson asked his mother as he paid for the brunch.

"No, but I want to. I saw the preview."

Judson and Amber rose from their chairs and so did Garland and Sydney. Garland twirled the carnation as she walked with them to the parking lot. She noticed Amber held hers as well. Judson opened the car door for all three: his mother, his wife and his daughter.

Garland sat with Sydney in the back seat and talked with her about the books she'd read lately as they rode to the movie theatre.

Soon they were there, Judson parked as close as he could and all four waked to the ticket booth together. The lady in the booth handed Judson the tickets and they headed for the concession stand.

Garland inhaled the scent of fresh popped popcorn as she waited in line. "I'll get a large popcorn to share with Sydney."

"Okay," Sydney said.

Judson looked at Sydney. "Nana, can't have a lot of salt or butter on her popcorn because she has high blood pressure. So you can't put all that stuff on it."

Garland looked at him, then Sydney. "I can. I can put butter on it. Yes, I can."

"I love popcorn," Sydney said. "That's why I don't want braces, you can't eat popcorn for three years. You don't understand, I inhale popcorn."

Garland laughed. She ordered a soft drink for her and a sprite for Sydney.

Sydney called out, "Soda hi five." She raised her arm and bumped her cup together

with Garland's.

Garland and Sydney followed Judson and Amber down the hall, lined with arcade machines, to theatre 19.

All four sat in the comfortable theatre seats, pulled their phones out and shut them off at the same time.

Garland turned toward Sydney, "You programmed my number into your phone, right?"

"Yes." Sydney's tone revealed that she thought it was a

dumb question. She stuffed a handful of popcorn in her mouth.

As the movie previews played all four of them gave their ratings at the end of each one by turning their thumbs either up or down.

"I like Christina Ricci," Garland said as the actual movie began.

"Me too," Amber agreed.

"I don't know who that is." Sydney shook the bag of popcorn. "I don't want to watch this movie. Let's see a different one."

"This is what we're seeing and this is all we're seeing, "Amber said.

"Christina Ricci's in this, isn't she?" Judson asked.

"Yes, she is." Garland took a sip of her drink. Then she reached over to the bag Sydney held and scooped up a handful of popcorn. The fresh, salty, buttery taste had her licking her lips.

The film showed warm-hearted experiences of motherhood from different

characters' viewpoints. It had Garland thinking about her own memories of motherhood.

It had been a wonderful life since Judson was born. She recalled her childhood. And all of the physical violence. She remembered the time her father literally beat her senseless, she fell unconscious during the five-hour spanking, that was what he falsely called it. He had told her then that he was trying to kill her. He wanted her to die. She was six at the time.

The next day she had told the teacher, who had responded by saying she was a bad girl to tell lies about her father. Her mother always dressed her in tights and a dress, so the bruises didn't show, as he'd hit her on her inner legs. The bruises on her body that

did show were attributed to her being clumsily and bumping into things. That's what her parents had told the school and they believed them.

She survived many attacks that almost killed her. But she continued to adopt the belief that her parents just didn't know better. That they were people who didn't know how to love and she had to forgive them. This is what other people always told her.

But at Judson's birth, she realized she couldn't do one single thing to her son that they had done to her. She knew then that they were not simply uncaring people, they were abusers with clear intent.

It was at Judson's birth that Garland's first repressed memories of sexual abuse were set free. She realized the lies her parents told about her and all the things they'd done were for the sole purpose of making it easier for her father to get by with raping her. Her mother handled the cover up part. She'd made a phone call when that realization had hit her and confronted her mother. And her response to Garland about her father raping her, the first time at age four, was, "Well he didn't know what to do with a little girl."

That was when the truth dawned on her. Nothing they had done had anything to do with her. These people were pedophiles. Their abuse of her and connection to her was no different than a predator who kidnaps a child and hurts them. And she realized then that other than the birth part, these people weren't her parents, they were her abusers. She'd never had an actual mother.

However, at that moment she resolved to be one... a good mother to her son. As Judson's mother, she learned what it was to have a beautiful mother and child bond for the first time in her life. Judson never knew anything less. For Garland, books and magazines on parenting took the place of family advice and good experiences to pull from. They gave her all the information she needed on discipline, potty training, the best toys, explaining the birds and the bees, and so much more.

As far as babysitters and nurseries, Garland was vigilant and wary. She didn't put up with people treating Judson badly. Anger, still held inside from her childhood, rose in her at those times. She got emotional quite a bit with the school district. She insisted they follow federal and state policies like they were supposed to, so Judson would get the equal education he was entitled to, despite his dyslexia.

Garland wished she had more earning potential and hadn't been so poor. As a call center customer service representative, she'd put up with a long line of unprofessional bosses in addition to customers yelling and cursing her out daily on the phone. She kept a photo of Judson on her desk at work, and glancing at the big smile on his face during the day is what always got her through. But she worked so hard for so little.

Garland regretted Judson's hard life, having to ride the bus and the few times they did have cars they were old junk ones that broke down. She couldn't afford to fix them. Yet he had grown up well and he had made a better life for himself than what she was able to give him economically. She'd given him a good life emotionally—filled with love and he'd given her a loving family in turn.

TEXAS 1993

Garland parked on the side of the road and with Judson

in his white baseball uniform and cap, glove in hand, she walked with him up to the field. The other kids were on the sidelines with the coach and that's where Judson ran to.

Garland sat down on the bleachers by the other parents on her son's team, The Lions. She'd noticed most of the parents at the games were fathers, except for the Ramirez's, both mother and father, always came for their son, Jose.

Mrs. Ramirez said, "Happy Mother's Day."

"Happy Mother's Day to you too." She smiled back at her.

Garland said 'Hi,' to Joe's father and Devon's father as well, they both sat near her on the bleachers.

The game started with Judson's team up to bat. Garland shouted, "Go Lions!" When any of the boys from the Lions hit the ball and got on base, she yelled, "Way to go."

Garland couldn't believe Judson was already eleven, he was really growing up. The opportunity to play sports with other boys helped Judson learn stuff that Garland just didn't know, being the girly-girl that she was. She'd never liked sports. But she loved watching Judson play sports. He enjoyed baseball and his friends on the team. His coach and all the parents were great.

Another woman sitting near Garland, but on the bottom bleacher, was yelling encouragement for the kids as well. That's what it seemed like to Garland.

The enthusiastic woman grew louder and more vocal. Garland was so captivated by the game and Judson and his friends, she didn't pay much attention to her

The Ramirez's called to Garland, "Mrs. Scot, come up here with us."

Garland stood and walked up the bleachers to sit with them.

Jose's father leaned closer to her and whispered, "I didn't want you sitting near that lady."

"She's scary." Jose's mother rolled her eyes.

"Who is she?" Garland saw the lady wasn't sitting any longer.

The loud woman was animated, she moved her arms a lot and paced back and forth

in front of the bleachers as she shouted to someone.

Jose's mother shrugged her shoulders. "She's the mother of a kid on the other team."

"The one we're playing against? I thought the parents for that team sat on the bleachers on the other side."

"She came over here." Jose's father said.

Garland gazed at the woman, who kept yelling. Her speech even seemed slurred.

Garland watched the tall referee walk over to the lady and tell her, "You need to be quiet or you'll be asked to leave. This a YMCA game and we don't allow anything but good sportsmanship." Garland hadn't even noticed how the woman had been yelling at the referee and the kids on the Lion's team. She'd just thought the lady was cheering the kids on like she was.

At that moment Judson was up to bat and she watched as he hit the ball dead on. She leapt to her feet. "Go Judson, go!"

He made it to first base. The coach came over and climbed up the bleachers to sit next to her. "He's doing good," he said in his deep, warm voice.

"Yes. Thank you so much for coaching him and the other kids." "I love it. You know, I told them they shouldn't schedule this game on Mother's Day but it's the only time they could fit it in."

"No it's fine. I like spending Mother's Day watching Judson play."

"Good." A frown came over his face and he cocked his head. "I saw you moved away from that other mother. Did she say or doing anything to you?"

"No, Jose's parents asked me to sit with them because they thought she might bother me."

"On the way out of the park, she hit the referee." The coach scowled.

"What?" What kind of parent hits a referee at a kids' baseball game, Garland thought?

The coach laughed. "Yeah. They've had trouble with her before."

"Oh, no."

"Her son's still playing, She's out in her car waiting for him because they won't let er back in the park."

"I would think not. She hit the referee?" Garland said.

"Yeah." He let out another good-natured chuckle.

Tom's father climbed up the bleachers and sat beside her as well. They both looked at Garland.

"We have something we wanted to ask you," the coach said.

Is there a problem? Judson had been able to play and get his uniform for free due to qualifying for a need-based scholarship. Had they run out of funds and had to cancel the scholarship? She wrung her hands. He obviously wanted to ask her something important. Both he and Tom's father had come over here.

The coach smiled. "We want to ask you if you would consider being our Team Mom?"

Her heart filled with warmth and joy. "I'd love to." Judson would be so happy.

Tom's father had as big a smile on his face as the coach did.

She looked up to see that Tom had just hit the ball and Judson ran to third base. Then Tom made it all the way to second. She and Tom's father both shot up from their seats and cheered.

CHAPTER 4

Texas 2016

Garland still twirled the pink carnation in her age spotted hand as she followed Judson, Amber, and Sydney into their house. They went there after the movie.

Her baby boomer feet moved a little slower than the those of her millennial and gen Z off spring, so she was the last to the door or the rotten egg as the old childhood saying goes.

As soon as she stepped inside, three dogs rushed her in a happy charge, yapping loudly with their tails waging. All excited to see their nana. The biggest one, the shepherd puppy, Violet, jumped up on her hind legs to greet Garland and got her claw hooked on the lace in Garland's dress. She had to carefully unhook the puppy's claw. The terriers, Jelly and Lenny were boys, and older and smaller. But all three loved Nana. Surrounded by dogs, she made her way to the sofa and plopped down.

Judson came from the hall where he had turned the home alarm off. He held a box gift-wrapped in yellow paper with a huge purple bow.

He sat beside her on the sofa. "Happy Mother's Day."

She set the carnation aside on the end table. "You shouldn't have. You took me to brunch and a movie. That was enough."

"Mom, aren't you going to unwrap you gift?" Amber asked as she sat in the chair next to the sofa.

"I helped pick it out." Sydney came and sat beside Judson.

Violet jumped up to sniff at the wrapped present.

Garland petted her, "This isn't for you."

She smiled at Amber. "Did you wrap this?"

"Yes. Judson can't wrap gifts." Amber flashed a big grin at her husband.

"Amber wrapped it," he said.

Garland pulled out the big purple bow and tore into the bright yellow paper. She

opened the white cardboard box and pulled out a gorgeous hand-carved bowl etched with wood-burned Celtic knot work. "It's the one the guy made at the Houston Highland Games." She ran her fingers across the mystical Celtic knots. The wood was so smooth, carved to perfection. "You must have got it yesterday when you and Sydney helped with my booth...with selling my books."

"Do you like it?" Judson asked.

"I Love it. It's incredible. But this was expensive."

"No, it was reasonable. He made it by hand. The guy who made it told me that before there was a written language they used the Celtic knots almost like a language."

"It's the most beautiful bowl I've ever seen." Joy buoy-antly rose in her. It was the perfect gift.

"Look Mom, when you have your book signings you can use this to put your book marks in."

Garland smiled at Judson. "It's wonderful." He was so thoughtful.

"I helped pick it out," Sydney said again.

Garland reached over Judson to give her granddaughter a big hug. She pulled Judson into her arms for a huge bear hug. She released Judson's embrace and walked over to Amber and wrapped her arms around her as well.

"I've got the best family in the whole world," Garland said.

2000 TEXAS

"I did it." Judson smiled. "Graduating class of 2000."

"I'm so excited," Garland said.

This was the best Mother's Day she'd had so far because it was also the day her baby was graduating from high school.

The school chose to hold the ceremony on a Sunday so all the parents, who worked weekdays or Saturdays could come. She turned into the school lot and parked, then she and Judson stepped out of the car.

She fixed her gaze on her son in his royal blue, flat cap with the gold tassel and the gown falling about boot level above his slacks. "You look so good." So tall...so handsome... my baby...grown up. She almost burst with excitement.

As they walked toward the auditorium, she said, "Ed is coming. He called right before we left."

Garland never remarried but she managed to get a big brother from the big brother and sister program for Judson when he was eight.

"That's good. He's a good big brother."

They walked inside and Garland could hardly believe it. "This place is almost full."

"There are so many people." Judson looked around, then pointed to the handmade deigns showing where the students should go.

Garland pointed to some empty seats she saw on the floor of the auditorium. "I'm going to sit over there. If you can't find me when it's over, we'll meet right outside the

door by that tree we passed coming in."

"I love you, mom." Judson gave her a tight hug and headed toward the front of the auditorium to sit with the other graduates.

Garland found a seat and then heard someone call her name. She looked up to see Ted. "How did you find me?"

"I was standing around looking for a seat when I saw you sit down here."

"Wow, that worked out great. Judson's up front with the kids, the other graduates."

Ed nodded.

"Class of 2000...can you believe it?" Garland intertwined her fingers and pressed her

hands to the base of her neck.

"No, and I can't believe how big this is. This is much larger than my high school graduation."

"Mine too." Garland looked around. All the seats were full. Then she gazed at the stage as the principal, a tall man with a touch of gray in his dark hair, stepped up to the podium.

His deep voice carried through the intercom to everyone as he spoke about the fine young people here today and the opportunities ahead for them.

Garland clapped along with everyone else as she

thought of Judson. What a good boy he was, what a good man he'd become.

The auditorium grew silent as the school choir walked on stage. A blonde kid about Judson's age took a seat at the piano and began to play.

Goose bumps prickled on Garland's arms as the choir sang, "You raise me up to more than I can be."

She thought, I raised him but he also raises me up all the time.

When the choir finished, the principal returned to the stage. As he called out each name, students walked up one by one and he handed them their diploma.

A thrilling joy sang in every vein in Garland's body as Judson accepted his diploma and shook the principal's hand. She glanced at Ted and the huge smile on his face heightened her pride and happiness even more.

It seemed that the ceremony was over and Judson was by her side in no time at all.

"Hi, mom. I got it." He held his diploma high in a champion type pose.

"Wait, let me snap a picture." Garland dug into her purse for her camera and took the photo as quick as she could. "Got it." She stuffed the camera back in her handbag. "I am so proud of you. Look...Ted came."

Still clutching his diploma in one hand, Judson open his arms and hugged Ted. Then he released Ted from his embrace and turned to Garland. "Here mom, this is for you."

He handed her his diploma.

"I'm so proud of you." A warm happy sensation spread through her as she glanced at the little blue folder that held his diploma inside.

"Take that home for me," Judson said.

"You're coming with me, aren't you?" Garland asked.

"My friends are here, Elizabeth, Chris, Richard, Carlos, they're all sitting over there."

He pointed to the other side of the auditorium.

"I'm so glad they could come. That's great. Are they coming over here?"

Ted spoke up. "I'd like to take you and your mom out to dinner to celebrate."

"Oh, how nice," Garland said.

"What?" Judson's eyebrows knitted together and his brow wrinkled as his lips turned down into a frown.

She assumed he just hadn't heard. "Ted's going to take you and me out for a graduation dinner."

Judson seemed to stiffen as he crossed his arms over his chest. "Okay, but I have to tell my friends. I'll meet you outside by the car."

He walked away and Garland didn't think much of it.

She and Ted went outside to wait for Judson. They chatted about how they'd been, and about how great Judson was doing as they stood by the tree out front. She glanced t the manicured lawn and the tall silver pole with the flag flapping in the spring breeze.

She glanced at Ted. "Such nice weather today, not hot like usual."

"Yes, it's such a beautiful day," Ted said.

This would be the last day she and Judson would ever come here to Sharpstown High School. Garland took a long, slow breath, then she looked back at the school and saw Judson walking toward them.

Ted smiled at him and then at Garland. "Do you like steak? There's this great steak house nearby and they have chicken fried steak too."

"Yes, chicken fried steak and mashed potatoes is

Judson's favorite," Garland answered, but she also noticed that Judson didn't say anything.

"We can take our own cars, you can follow me in yours to the restaurant," Ted said.

Garland agreed and she walked with Judson to their car and got in. She started the engine and pulled out behind Ted's car and began following it to the restaurant.

"I'm really mad at you, Mom."

"Mad. Why?" What had she done?

"My friends and I were going to get together after the ceremony. That's why they were there. And now I can't be with my friends because I have go to dinner with Ted."

"Why didn't you tell me you made plans?" She had to remember he was 18, friends were more important than anyone at that age. Also teenagers never told their parents too much about their plans.

"I didn't know Ted was even coming."

"He called right before we left, to let us know he could make it. He's been part of your life since you were eight years old. He deserves to share this with you."

"You should have asked me," Judson said.

"Maybe so, but you should have told me you had plans." Garland pulled into the parking lot of the restaurant right behind Ted. She undid her seat belt and leaned toward Judson. "It's my fault you're not with your friends, Ted doesn't know. It was so kind of him to invite us to dinner. Please be as nice as you can. Enjoy yourself, have a good time. You can spend the rest of the evening with your friends. You hardly ever see Ted now that you're grown."

"I know how to act but I'd rather be with my friends." He got out of the car. She nodded at him and said, "I know."

Garland walked up to Ted, Judson followed, and they all entered the steak house together. The hostess seated them at a table with a crisp white tablecloth and soon the waiter took their order.

Ted turned to Judson. "So, this is a big day."

"It just graduation. Everyone graduates from high school." Judson rolled his eyes.

Garland gazed at Judson as she handed him her cell phone. "Why don't you call your friends and let them know you'll meet up with them after dinner."

Judson shrugged. "Okay." He took the phone and went outside to make the call.

"He's worked so hard, he really deserves this. Is he going to college?"

"He got a grant to take come classes at the community college to get a computer certificate and he may go on to get a degree out of it, but he'll have to get a student loan and he doesn't want to do that." She shrugged. She wished she could pay for college. She felt that she'd let him down. "He's working now, as a distributor. He likes it." She knew her smile must have spread ear to ear, she was so proud of her son.

Judson sat back down. He must have heard what his mother said because he looked at Ted and said, "I deliver potato chips to grocery stores and make displays. I like making the displays. I like to build them as high as I can."

"That sounds like fun." Ted grinned.

The waiter brought the food and the drinks. Garland cut off a slice of her chicken fried steak. She and Judson had always been a family but it wasn't just them. It was also Ted and Judson's friends. They were all part of Judson's family. They had all contributed to the man he'd become.

"By the way," Ted said, "Happy Mother's Day."

"Happy Mother's Day," Judson reached over to hug her.

They ate their food and said bye to Ted. Soon they were on their way home.

Garland walked with Judson into the house, and while he changed to go out with his friends, she opened up a chest she'd decoupage to put treasures in. She placed the cap, gown and diploma inside it. That's when she saw the letter she'd put there. The last one she'd gotten from Samuel.

She closed her eyes as she thought, he's old enough to see this now. Just as he hung up the phone, she walked into the kitchen. "This is the last letter your father sent." She held it out to him.

"What?" Judson rubbed his forehead. "How long ago?"

"Two years."

"He hasn't written you since?"

"I'm thinking that's not his fault. He stopped writing last time because he said I didn't write him back. But I did. He never got my letter. And I'm thinking that must have happened again. The borders in Iran are closed and sometimes it's hard to get mail through."

"What does he say?" Judson crossed his arms over his chest.

"Apparently, he had such a hard time dealing with not ever seeing you again he had to go to a doctor. Though he is working as a civil engineer there now. That's good."

"He didn't have to leave me."

"No, he didn't. Even though we divorced, he could have gotten a job, stayed here...been a part of your life. I think he realizes that now."

"Well, it's his loss"

"It is. A great loss."

Judson moved closer to her. "Mom, I'm sorry that I got mad about having dinner with Ted."

"No, I just wish I had known about your plans then I wouldn't have said yes to Ted."

"The country fried steak was so good." He flashed a wry grin.

"It was." She laughed.

"Well, I've got to go. I'm meeting my friends at the club." Judson hugged her tight. "I know I already told you, but happy Mother's Day."

"Happy graduation day." As he opened the door she called out, "Have fun and drive safe."

As Garland put the letter back in the chest she thought, Judson's right, Samuel messed up and missed out. But she didn't. She'd been here with her son to celebrate not only another fantastic Mother's Day but also the first day of Judson's adult life. "A great day indeed," she said aloud.

CHAPTER 5

Texas 2016

As he sat on the sofa next to her, Judson leaned closer. "Mom, we have one more surprise for you." The smile on Judson's face spread from ear to ear.

And the smile on Amber's face was just as big.

"Another surprise?" Now, she was even more excited. Her heart hammered. "What is it?"

"I've been saving up and we're taking a family vacation. We're going to Disney

world."

"Oh, that's wonderful." He'd found a way to take his wife and daughter to Disney World. She was so happy for him. It was an old dream she hadn't been able to fulfil—to take Judson to Disney World. She'd wanted to so bad when he was little. But she never had the money.

Amber got up and sat down next to her and said, "We want to take you too."

"Me? Disney World?"

Judson nodded. "The walking may be hard for you but you can go to the hotel room if you get tired."

"We're going to stay at the Polynesian Hotel. That's the one Judson wanted." Amber's eyes shined so bright.

"Oh, that's the famous one." Wow, her son was taking her to Disney World. "It's their best one." Judson grinned.

"I won't get tired. I can walk around Walt Disney World." Garland smiled back at him.

"We're not going until August, but we wanted you to know about it ahead of time so you'd be able to make plans."

"And to give you time to find someone to watch Severus," Amber said.

"It's going to be for a week, do you thinks someone can feed Severus for you?" Judson's eyebrows arched.

"Sure, I'll make sure Severus is taken care of."

"I'm going too," Sidney said.

"You're the main reason we're going." Amber put her arm around her daughter.

"Of course you're going you have to see Disney World." Garland smiled at her granddaughter.

"Nana, I have something for you too." She eased out of her mother's embrace and darted to her room.

She soon ran back to Garland with a card in her hand. "I made it for you in computer class."

Garland took the precious card. There was a flower on it she'd copied and pasted from online. Garland opened it up and read the message aloud, "To the best Nana in the world. One free hug for Mother's Day!"

Garland couldn't hold back any longer, tears burst from her. The card was better than Disney World. Though she'd love the magic kingdom she'd be happy anywhere if her family was with her.

"This card is gorgeous. The best mother's day present I've gotten. It's going up on my refrigerator door." She stood and took her free hug from Sydney.

Then she turned and gestured to Judson to stand. She pulled him into her arms. She held him as tight as she could then she said, "Judson," with every bit of joy and pride as when she declared his name to the doctor in that operating room so long ago, "I love you."

"I love you too, Mom."

She looked into his eyes, knowing hers were tearing up again. "I love you more."

Garland never had a real mother but she knew what a good mother was. She was a good mother. She'd raised a great son.

The End

DEAR READER

Dear Reader,

Thank you for reading I Love You More. I hope you enjoyed meeting Garland and Judson and learning their story. It was one of the stories in the box set Mother's Day Magic. It was fun and rearing to write a story that celebrates mothers and shined the spotlight on the strength and love of single moms. I am a single mom myself. To thank you for reading my story, I have included a bonus, fantasy, single mom story. It follows this thank you note. I hope you enjoy The Ghost Lights of Marfa.

Again, thank you so much for reading I Love You More. Readers like you make writing worthwhile.

Thank you so much,

Cornelia Amiri
   http://corneliaamiri.com/
   CelticRomanceQueen@gmail.com

Adventures of A Small Town Single Mom - Beamed To An Alternate Dimension. There mysterious aliens set Kristy on a path of self-exploration and romance. Is the wonderful world of In everything it seems to be? Or do the Inids have an ulterior motive for helping her and her son?

THE GHOST LIGHTS OF MARFA
by Maeve Alpin

A recorded sighting of the of ghost lights in Marfa, Texas was first published in 1957. Many claim observations of the lights go back at least to the 1800s. Ghost lights occur around the world, with orange the most common color. The Marfa lights are usually orange, red, white or yellow, but green and blue have been reported. In addition to numerous sightings, the lights have been documented many times in photographs and videos. Witnesses have posted homemade videos of the lights to YouTube. Every night, onlookers hoping to spot the lights, stop by the circular viewing center, located about eight miles east of Marfa, which includes a picnic area, restrooms, and a parking lot.

THE GHOST LIGHTS OF MARFA
by Cornelia Amiri

The car will die. And hungry . . . stranded . . . we'll die.

This thought blared in Kristy's head for the endless stretch of road she'd driven thorough the bare west Texas desert. Finally driving past the Welcome to Marfa sign, she released a sigh of relief.

"Are we there yet, Mommy?" Cody's high-pitched voice pulsed with energy.

"We sure are." Kristy glanced in the rear view mirror at her six-year-old son. Framed by two dimples, the corners of his rosy mouth turned up into a bright smile. His brown eyes snapped with merriment and dark curls fell across his forehead and his plump cheeks as he banged his plastic sword against the car seat. Cody couldn't have been happier and she wanted to keep it that way.

As a golden oldies station played *Bennie and the Jets*, she turned onto South Dean Street. "This is Marfa. We'll see the lights soon." She glanced at the fuel gauge. After a six-hour drive from San Antonio, it pointed near empty. "We made it."

"How do those lights come on?" Cody squeaked from the back seat. "What time do they come on?"

"Tonight, after it's dark."

The town reminded her of a western movie set as she drove by rows of white wooden houses and one-story adobe buildings. The peach-toned courthouse towered above them. Its gray dome caught her eye, along with its blanket of green lawn, adorned with bushy crepe myrtles and old pecan trees with sprawling branches. Driving down the narrow road, she soon spotted the white, rectangular building and the prominent black sign with white script, El Paisano.

"Cody, famous movie stars, James Dean, Rock Hudson, and Elizabeth Taylor slept in that hotel when they made *Giant* here, a real famous old movie."

"Who?" His brows arched over his wide brown eyes.

"You'll see it on TV one day, maybe on Turner Classic Movies. It doesn't matter, we're not staying there." *No money for that.* "We'll to camp out tonight, sleep in the car. Won't that be fun? I've got pillows in the trunk."

"I get to sleep in the car." He jerked his head, ruffling his mop of black hair.

"We're going to have so much fun, Cody."

As Kristy peered in the rearview mirror, she found the wide smile on his face contagious and her mood grew buoyant. She would try to get a job as a desk clerk or a maid at the El Paisano. Kristy had come to see the dusty ranch town as her last hope. In the middle of the vast desert, under the big Texas sky, Marfa —a place of consistency and peace, remained untouched by the economic crisis.

Just what she needed after discovering many family shelters only allow a month before they kick you out. You can't keep your children, if you can't feed them. Simple words, with *less* stuck on the end, like homeless, jobless, didn't explain all that. All the languages in the world can't explain that Mommy, the only person who takes care of you, can't. Lost her job and no one wants her. At six, you're on your own, in foster care. Kristy vowed that wouldn't happen to her son.

She glanced at a square, white building on West San

Antonio Street with El Cheapa in large, red script letters. "The town is so cute."

When the constable tacked the eviction notice to her apartment door, the only idea she came up with was to take Cody on a vacation. Show him the ghost lights of Marfa, the giant horseshoe, and the place James Dean made his last movie.

Like a rebel without a cause, she threw her kid and some clothes into the car and took off. She had nothing left but a few coins and dollar bills. What would it be, gas or food? Knowing eight dollars' worth of gas wouldn't get her far, she chose food.

"I'm hungry, Mommy." Cody opened his mouth wide signaling he was ready to eat.

She spotted the familiar white, red-roofed restaurant. "There's the Dairy Queen."

After parking, she finger-combed her shoulder-length, auburn hair. She retrieved a kohl pencil from her purse and lined her pale blue eyes, then brushed a coat of thick mascara on her long, thin lashes. She had to look good just in case. Maybe they were hiring there. *You never know.*

Cody unbuckled his seatbelt and scurried into the Dairy Queen with Kristy at his heels. He plopped onto the seat of a bright orange booth, as she asked the cashier if they had any openings.

She received the familiar reply. "Not at this time."

After ordering a junior hamburger and a kid's meal, Kristy gave into her cravings and ordered a watermelon slushy. The sweet, cool, refreshing treat was a favorite of hers since she was Cody's age and it didn't look like she'd be having another one anytime soon. So she decided to splurge. She ordered Cody one, too.

She sat in the booth and hungrily clutched her

hamburger. The moment she bit into the soft bun, the combined flavors of beef patty, ripe tomato slices, and lettuce wrapped around her tongue. As Kristy munched her burger, she reflected on how she'd ended up here.

When she found out she was pregnant with Cody, it was a shock. Though she took birth control pills, she'd missed a day. She never considered not keeping the baby, even when her boyfriend pulled the routine 'I don't want this, I don't think it's mine.' But he manned-up, and at six months into her pregnancy, a justice of the peace married them. The judge wished her the best of luck, but even then, she wondered if she was making a mistake. A year later, after her husband hit her for a third time, she escaped to a shelter for battered women. The divorce took all her savings and her ex-husband disappeared. She never received a single child support payment.

At school events or anywhere someone asked Cody to introduce his mother and father, he always said, "My mother and father is Kristy." That never failed to bring a warm flutter to her heart.

Then, she lost her job. She went to work on Friday, payday, and found the office locked. The owner skipped. Since it was a contract position, selling credit card machines to businesses, her boss didn't take out taxes, so she wasn't able to file for unemployment compensation.

Kristy managed the rent that month and a United Way charity paid it for her the next. The third month, her luck ran out. She still hadn't found a job.

Now, she'd spent her last dollar on fast food. But in the back of her mind, she believed the ghost lights of Marfa would bring her luck. *Something had to*, she thought.

As he finished the last of the slushy, Cody's noisy slurping brought her back from her musings.

"Mommy, is it time to see the lights?" He puckered his lips and strummed his finger across them, making a brrrrrr sound.

"Don't you want your treat?" She tore the coupon off the kiddy bag and used it to get the free chocolate-dipped ice cream cone. She handed it to Cody and piled a stack of napkins on the table. He grinned ear to ear, eagerly biting through the chocolate covering to the soft vanilla ice cream.

"I finished, Mommy." He popped the last piece of the kiddy cone into his chocolate-ringed mouth. "Are the lights ready to come on?"

Kristy grabbed a napkin and wiped his face. "First, I'm going to take you to see the world's biggest horseshoe. Would you like that?"

"Yes, yes." He climbed off the seat and jumped up and down. "Let's go."

She stood and grabbed her purse. "What a lucky boy you are, Cody. You get to see the giant horseshoe now and the ghost lights tonight." She spotted the toy on the table. "Don't forget your sword."

He ran back, grabbed the pirate sword and darted to the car. Kristy buckled him in and slid behind the wheel. She fit the key into the ignition and took off down the quiet, traffic free street. She drove past a row of small adobe houses, and then spotted a looming wall with an old army barracks rising above it. "See that Cody? Soldiers lived there a long time ago. Now they keep famous art in it."

"I want to go there." Cody bounced on the backseat.

She turned the corner and parked the car in the lot. They jumped out and rushed toward the twenty-foot tall horseshoe.

Her gaze scanned the rough, dark brown surface and

locked on the huge, bent nail stuck through the shoe. Kristy understood how the nail felt.

"It's so big, Mommy." Cody's eyes grew wide and his face beamed. "What kind of horse would that fit?"

She laughed aloud. It had been days since she'd done that. "A pretty big horse." What would she do without Cody? He was the one bright light in her life, she had to find a way to support him.

"I've never seen a giant horse." Cody wobbled his head.

"No, but you've seen a giant horseshoe."

"Yeah, I have. Wait 'til I tell the kids at school." He reached his tiny hand out and touched the end of the horse-shoe where it rested on its aluminum stand.

"Come, let's see the rest." Kristy grabbed his hand and they skipped toward the field scattered with huge concrete cubes.

She hadn't explained that he couldn't go back to his old school, that they couldn't go back to their old house. She couldn't bear for him to be afraid or worried. He didn't know anything was wrong and she was going to do her best to keep it that way as long as she could. Though time was running out. Right now she only had the car and the belong-ings in the trunk, nothing else.

"Mommy, they're big boxes."

"Yes . . . art."

As Cody ran in and out of the square sculptures, bran-dishing his pirate sword, Kristy waded through knee-high grass, past a stand of green, prickly-pear cactus. Her eyes drank in the panorama of the Mountains, sloping against ribbons of pink and amber, rippling across the vast sky. She tilted her head back, gazing at the sinking sun. As she breathed in the fresh desert air, the weight of a thousand tons pressed against the pit of her stomach, then vanished, leaving her refreshed and hopeful. Surely if there was any place where her luck could turn around, it was this tiny, enchanting town.

She glanced at Cody, sword-fighting with a cluster of juniper trees. "Look at the sunset, punkin."

The glowing orb floated over the gentle curve of the distant tanzanite-tinted mountains. "I wish this day would last forever." The clouds changed from white to bright pink, like clumps of cotton candy. "I love you, Cody."

"I love you too, Mommy."

"It's dark enough now. Let's go see those lights. I'll race you."

He reached the car first. She was still panting as she buckled him in, then she drove toward the observation deck.

On the way, her son sang an original Cody tune. "We're going to the lights. We're going to see the lights. We're going to see the magic lights, the magic lights of Marfa."

She rubbed her teeth against her lower lip as she glanced at the gauge, so close to empty. Kristy hoped she'd make it to the observation deck and back into town. Getting stranded on Highway 90 could ruin this vacation or what she called a vacation. But as the road stretched out before her, the observation deck seemed farther away than she anticipated.

"Mommy, where are the lights? I don't see them. Are they coming? I want to see the lights."

"I promise you, Cody, you'll see them. Bright, glowing lights in the sky. Like magic."

Kristy's body hummed with excitement. An orange light, the size of a basketball, appeared out of the darkness, then as if animated, the sphere zipped and zagged across the sky. "Cody, look." Suddenly, another light popped up. It blinked away as quickly as it appeared.

"Mommy, the lights turned on!"

"Yes they did, Cody. They sure did." Out of nowhere, multi-colored flashes of red, white, green, and yellow rollicked in the sky. "I don't have to drive to the observation deck. We can see them right here."

The glowing balls drew her like a lodestone. Kristy longed to be closer to them, to leap and dance in the night sky. She pulled the car to the side of the road. With her fingers flying against the buckle, she tore out of her seatbelt. Cody rushed out as well.

"Stay on this side of the car, punkin. It's dark and someone might run over you if you get out on that road."

"Mommy, look." His eyes grew wide with wonder as he pointed at the glowing lights, changing color and size. "Hello light, hello." Cody leapt up and down. "Look, Mommy, I can jump high enough to touch the lights." He stretched his arms over his head, reaching up with his fingers splayed, and bounced like a yo-yo.

"This is weird." Kristy watched the lights line up like a strand of beads and then scatter across the sky, as if they burst loose from a broken necklace. A beam of green popped off, then suddenly flashed back on. A blinking red orb whizzed back and forth across the fudge-colored sky.

Cody spread his skinny arms and spun like an airplane propeller. "Look Mommy, the lights and I are dancing together, them in the sky and me on the ground."

"Yes, I see. Look at you dance, just like the ghost lights." Kristy twirled like Cody, until she grew dizzy and stumbled.

"I used to do this as a little girl. I'd forgotten how much fun it is." Bubbling warmth filed her as she bounced and whirled, playing with Cody, dancing with the lights. As she gazed at a red light, it grew brighter and changed to yellow.

One of the green lights split into two. "How do they do that?"

"Mommy, I don't want to leave. Can't we stay with the lights forever?"

"They have to go back to where they came from. It's late, it'll be morning soon."

A brilliant orange light captured her gaze, expanding as it stalked toward them, looming closer and closer. She realized now, not a single car had driven past them.

"We need to head back. I'll let you leave the seatbelt off, just this once, so you can look out the rear window and watch the lights."

"No, I want to stay with the lights."

"You're tired. It's been a long day. You need to go to bed, punkin." She held the door to the back seat open as he protested, scuffing his feet against the dirt.

Finally, Cody climbed in. Kristy turned the key in the ignition, shifted the old clunker into drive. She originally planned to camp out in the car at the observation deck since they had restrooms there but now she realized they'd never make it on the gas she had left, so she decided to go back to town and find a good place to park for the night. She made a U-turn, but the eerie, orange light shadowed them.

Kneeling, facing the rear window, Cody watched the orange orb hovering above the car. "Mommy the light likes me. It's going to camp out with us."

"It's not following us, Cody, it can't. It just looks like it is."

"It is so following us. Mommy, I see it."

With no other cars on the highway, Kristy braked to a stop. "Let me show you." She threw the car into reverse and drove backwards. "See, Cody. If it was following us, it would move back just like it moved forward, but–" She noticed the light stayed directly above them. "Oh no! Shit! It is following us." She pulled to a stop.

Her hands shook on the steering wheel. "This can't be happening."

"The light likes me, Mommy. Can it come home with us?" Cody shook his plastic sword at the light. "To play with me."

"No, punkin, it's a light in the sky. It can't go anywhere with us. And it can't hurt us. Whether it follows us or not, it's only a bright light. It can't do anything." Her breathing grew shallow. She shifted back into drive and sped forward.

"Look, Mommy, it stays with us. When you go fast, it goes fast, and when you go slow, it goes slow. Mommy, why are you stopping?"

"Oh no." The fuel gauge pointed past the E. The car came to a complete stop. "Damn." She smacked the steering wheel, pushed the gearshift to park, clicked off the headlights, and switched on the emergency blinkers. "We're out of gas." She trembled as shrill, yipping howls of coyotes sliced through the night air. "Don't worry, Cody, it will be okay."

"Mommy, if the car won't go, we get to stay with the light."

"Yes, the light's still here. Just like us." She gazed at the orange ball hovering above them. "You're no help at all. Some magic you are."

Suddenly, the ghost light descended, drawing closer and closer to earth, like a paper kite that lost its wind. "Cody, jump out, now!" Kristy shoved the car door open.

She leapt out as did Cody and she pulled him to the side of the road with her. The orange light surrounded the stranded car.

"Mommy, the light's coming to ride with us."

"That car is out of gas, it's not going anywhere, not even for a ghost light." She bit her lip to hold back a scream.

The orange dome enveloped the old clunker. Just like that, the headlights popped on. The car honked by itself, repetitively. Windows rolled up and down on their own. The trunk flapped open and closed, like a bird's wing. An old Sinatra song about flying away blared on the car radio.

"No!" Her heart beat so hard it nearly leapt out of her chest. "This can't be happening." She grabbed Cody's hand and yanked him further away from the car and the light. "It's not right, we've got to get away." Her foot slid on a rock in the ground, as she fell, his fingers slipped out of her grasp. "Cody, no!"

As he rushed to the light, Kristy let out a terrified scream, "Cody!"

Petrified with fear, she watched her small, wiry son, dart into the dome of light. She managed to push herself up. "Help! Someone help!"

Cody went still. "The light loves us, Mommy." His whole face, beamed with pure joy. "I want to stay with it."

"Cody, get away. Come to me, now."

Caught in the light, glowing with happiness, he didn't seem to hear his mother.

She reached out her arms, intent on grabbing her son and pulling him free of the freaky ghost light. "Cody, please." She dashed into the light to save her baby.

The moment her foot slid into the light, complete, utter peace flooded her. She'd never felt such deep joy, even at the happiest moment of her life, when Cody was born. Kristy didn't want to leave the light. Instead of grabbing Cody, she wrapped her arms around him in a tight hug.

"I want to stay." His beaming smile echoed in his exuberant voice

She squeezed him tighter. "Yes, of course we're staying in the light."

Mother and child lovingly embraced, standing beside the car in the center of the radiant glow, basking in its rapt warmth. The light blinked, then it vanished with Kristy and Cody.

***

Kristy squeezed Cody's hand and gasped with shock as blue-skinned beings strolled past, on a street paved in a gleaming silver material.

"Cody, I think you're dreaming or I'm dreaming or we're both dreaming." Now daylight, a yellow orb, like the sun, along with two white moons, one small, one huge, hung in the pale green sky. "This can't be real."

As she squeezed Cody's hand, he reached out with his other and pinched her.

Kristy yelped. "Cody, stop it!"

"You're not dreaming, Mommy." He placed his hand on his hip. "Why are they blue?"

Blue people with wide, square heads clustered around, jabbering in an unfamiliar language.

"Where are we?" She slapped her hand to the shallow below her throat. "Another planet?"

"Actually, another dimension, our world is called In." A blue man, whose head took up a third of his body size, smiled. "Are you from the Lipan Apache Band? I not only speak English, I also know Apache, as well as 35 other terrestrial languages. I am a professor of Earth Studies." He bobbed his flat, turquoise head. "My name is Yog."

"What?" A surge of ice crusted fear shot through Kristy. "I'm not an Apache and I just speak English."

"Not Apache? Then you may not know the Hactcin are the creators of both In and Earth. You must have fallen on hard times. The Hactcin send the lights to help anyone in that area, in the Apache territory, who have bad luck."

Even the lights have it in for me. "What happens here? Is it some kind of purgatory, I'm to be punished for having bad luck?" Her body shook and her legs went, as limp as boiled pasta. "And why is Cody here, he hasn't done anything wrong?" She pushed Cody behind her. She wasn't about to let that blue stranger touch her child.

"Oh no, what happens is your luck turns around, of course. That's the whole purpose, to give you and your son a second chance here on In."

Kristy's fingers shook as she tucked a strand of auburn hair behind her ear. "The orange light beamed us up?"

"Yes, the lights are portals and porters all in one, finding those who are worthy of good luck." His rectangular lips spread into a wide, toothy smile. "If you go to the council office, they will help you with everything you need."

"Mommy, this place is cool. How did you bring us here?"

"I don't know, even though Yog explained it." She shrugged to hide her shock and fear from Cody and shifted her gaze back to the blue professor. "You're not human."

"No, in this dimension we are called Inids." Yog pointed to a one story, flat roofed building. "They will explain all."

"I can't go in there. I left my purse in the car with my ID and our birth certificates." Kristy knew of the long list of documents you had to bring, she'd heard stories about people who'd spent all day in the immigration office only to be told to come back and bring more paperwork. The building looked just like one on Earth so surely the procedures wouldn't be too different.

Yog blinked his black eyes. "If the light brought you, the council has already given their permission and approval."

"Ok, that's convenient." Kristy took Cody's hand. "Come on, punkin." They strolled into the white, stone building and up to the counter, where a blue-skinned woman worked. She glanced down at Cody. "Stay next to me and don't let go of my hand. I don't know anything about these blue people... or beings...whatever they are."

The square-headed lady babbled something, but paused when Kristy didn't answer. "Oh, you don't speak Inish. That will have to be corrected," she said in English and pointed to a box on the counter, gesturing Kristy to peer into it.

"What is this, a vision test machine like the ones at the department of motor vehicles?" Kristy pressed her eyes against the lens in the box, a bright light flashed and her scalp tingled. "What was that?"

"A language upgrade. It's a type of mind enhancement." Instantly, she could speak and understand Inish.

The large-headed woman pulled two turquoise necklaces out of a drawer.

"You both need to wear one of these, unless you want to have your flesh dyed blue, like ours. You see, the color will bring you luck." The woman glared at her. "Your skin is very pink, isn't it? That's odd." The lady reached out her long blue fingers to touch Kristy's skin.

Kristy jumped back. "Yes, it is and no, we don't want to dye our skin. We'll wear the necklaces." Kristy slipped one of the silver chains, dangling a wire wrapped apache tear, around her neck and the other around Cody's.

She shifted her gaze back to the blue woman. "Since I'm new here, I'll need a place to stay until I can find a job, is there a family shelter for my son and I?"

"The council will provide housing for you, we consider you a very important person. The accommodations provided do not require any financial compensation on your part, you will be allotted full citizenship and a monthly allowance."

"Government housing, I don't know." She sighed. "I guess for now. Maybe I can get a job soon and get us a better place." She leaned closer to the woman. "How much is this monthly allowance?"

"Twenty thousand a month in your currency, American dollars, I believe."

Kristy crossed her arms. "Ma'am, I think there may be some mistake in that calculation."

"If it is not enough, we can offer more." The woman pointed to a thin, blue man. "He will escort you to your new home and see that you have everything you need."

"I'll go with the blue guy. But if it's a bad place or dangerous, I'm not staying. I have my son to think of." Holding Cody's hand, Kristy followed the man out of the building and down the street.

"Why are we stopping here, Mommy?"

The square-headed man flashed a wide, rectangular smile. "This is your house." The man pointed to a huge mansion, which took up a whole block.

Kristy's jaw fell open, she stared, speechless.

Cody let go of her hand and darted inside. Before she reached the door, he dashed back out and ran to her. "Mommy, I think it's a mall."

The slender, blue man led them into a marbled foyer. "Your house, and all that is in it, has been fashioned after a nice Earth home."

"How many people live here?" she asked the blue man. "Do we have our own room?"

"This home is just for you and your son of course. You have all the rooms."

Kristy glanced up at a glistening crystal chandelier.

"I hope the home and all the furnishings are satisfactory." Their guide gestured to her to follow him. "We've added toys and novelties to accommodate your child."

"Oh, good, if it's not too much trouble, he needs a plastic sword." Kristy took Cody by the hand as they trailed behind the blue man.

"I left my sword in the car, Mommy."

"Yes." Kristy gasped as they entered the first room. Her gaze scanned the video games, pool table, and an air hockey table.

Cody dashed to a racing game and spun the steering wheel back and forth. "Look Mommy, you don't need tokens or money, it's free."

Her senses reeled as she left Cody to play, and followed the blue guy into the other rooms, which held a full basketball court, an indoor swimming pool, a bowling alley, a skating rink, and a skateboard ramp.

"Cody's playrooms take up the entire first floor." She took a deep breath.

"Mommy, I won the game." Cody ran up to her.

"Good, punkin." Kristy had to ask her guide the obvious question. "What's upstairs?"

The blue man led her and Cody up the winding staircase and into a movie theatre. She stared wordlessly at the huge screen and rows of seats. Next, he showed her a dining room as large as most restaurants. Her heart hammered as they entered the library, lined with shelves, crammed with books.

When she glanced at her guide he nodded his head, anticipating her question before she asked it, he said, "They are earth books. In English."

Her mind spun with excitement, as she followed their

guide to the bedrooms. Both of them had large closets full of clothes and shoes. Hers included a salon area with makeup and a cosmetologist's table and chair.

"A hairdresser will come once a week to do your hair and nails." The blue man smiled.

"Wow." She couldn't even speak then a disturbing thought crossed heir mind. "But no blue nails and no blue hair."

"If that is your choice."

"Yes. And no dying our skin blue."

"As you wish."

The man called forth, and introduced her to, a staff of twenty servants.

Cody pointed to the row of blue servants." Mommy, are they going to watch me while you go to your new job?"

Kristy rubbed his head, gently tousling his soft, black hair. "Right now, here on In, I get to stay home with you. I don't have to go to work."

"Mommy, that's the best thing in the whole word."

"Getting to spend time with my little man is the best thing in *this* world and the one we came from, the best thing in *all* the worlds, Cody."

She'd been nearly hopeless, until she turned off US-67 and drove into a dusty ranch town, which led to the fulfillment of all her dreams. All that was missing was a dreamy man. Of course, he'd probably be blue.

"Mommy, I'm hungry."

She turned and smiled at the row of blue skinned women and men. "One of you must be a cook. Please show me to the pantry or refrigerator, wherever you keep the food. I need to learn the more important things about this world."

"Maybe they eat blue worms, that would be cool," Cody said.

She clutched her stomach. "Maybe not." As she trailed behind a plump, square-faced woman, Kristy's mouth watered for a hamburger.

At the chime of a bell, a servant dashed downstairs to the front door. Kristy followed, to see who'd come to visit. Her eyes froze on the tall, athletic physique of a human man, about 25. His thick, black hair tapered to the scooped neck of his Earth imported T-shirt and his muscles rippled under the jersey fabric.

"Hello, you must be the new arrivals from Earth." His generous mouth curved into a disarming smile.

Her pulse raced. "Yes, I am Kristy Travis." She smiled as Cody ran up. "And this is my son."

"My name is Nick, I'm so excited to see you." Compelling electric-blue eyes gleamed from his oval face. "You can teach me about my home planet."

Kristy imagined pressing her lips to his as he wrapped his sinewy arms around her and pulled her tight against the muscles of his broad chest. Her breath grew shallow. "What do you want to know about Earth?"

"Everything. You've heard of abandoned children. When I was four, someone, I guess one or both of my parents, stopped on Highway 90 and put me out of the car, right there on the road. That night, one of the lights brought me here. An Inid family adopted me as soon as I got here. I love my In parents, they're great, but I've always wondered about earth and what it's like to live there."

"I'll be glad to fill you in, if your wife won't mind?" She peered at him intently, waiting for his response.

"Oh, I'm not married." His blue eyes grew amused and

his lips twitched with humor. "While I'm here, is there is anything I can do to help you get settled?"

She moistened her lips with her tongue. "As a matter of fact, come with me to the kitchen to find something that tastes like cheeseburgers." As Kristy climbed the stairs, she forgot all about food and thought only of hungrily, covering his mouth with hers and tasting the sultry heat of Nick's full, firm lips.

***

Her arm brushed across his as they walked up the steps together. A hot shiver shot through him. He always thought he'd be alone. With his appearance so weird, so ugly compared to all the other people on IN, a small oval head, his skin a frightening, monstrous color, and on top of all that he was a giant. Still he'd resisted having his skin dyed blue. Something didn't seem quite right about posing as a native Inid when he was Earth born. He'd never been thrilled with that decision until today. He wasn't alone anymore, there were two others now, Kristy and her son. He wasn't ugly or weird he was just an earthling. Kristy head was small and her skin was a light tan shade as well. And she was beautiful. He couldn't keep his eyes off her.

Her smile made him feel so light, happy. Her eyes held a gleam of interest but he wasn't sure what to say or to do. He'd never mated with a woman before. The only In women who'd seemed interested in him were extremely experienced in sex and seemed curious about what he was like in that manner.

Something about putting her in this house, supposedly fashioned after the ones on Earth, and fulfilling her every whim seemed strange. He had to tell her about his suspicions. First he had to show her what he thought was going on. If his suspsious were true, he feared she'd get upset. She might want to leave, return to earth. He didn't know if she could or if he could. If the Inids forced her to stay, she probably wouldn't want anything to do with them. She might not want anything to do with him either. Still it was better she found out now and that he was the one to show her. Hopefully, he was wrong and the Inids were genuinely being kind and generous to her. He rubbed his forehead.

They stepped into the kitchen. He walked over to a cabinet and hit an icon picture. Suddenly a little door opened and a pile of what looked like ground meat slid out on a plate.

Her eyebrows arched in a baffled expression.

"It keeps the food cold. This is *woch*, ground meat from a bird we eat a lot of here in In. It's the only meat we eat. I hope it taste like the cheeseburgers you're used to."

He set the plate under a little hood above the counter and clicked switch. In under a minute, the food looked completely cooked, though it had a grayish tint to it. He hit a button on the cabinet and six pieces of what look like bread came out. He pulled a spoon out of a drawer and spooned the *woch* onto three slices of bread then put another slice on top.

"Just like an earth sandwich. But what does it taste like?" Kristy asked.

"Try it." He smiled.

She took a small bite. "Not quite hamburger but it will do." She turned to her son. "Here, try this." She handed him a plate.

Cody bit into it. "It's good but I wanted blue worms."

"What?" Nick asked.

"Nothing." Kristy shrugged. "Don't mind him."

He moved his head closer to Kristy so he couldn't be overheard by anyone but her, in case his suspicions were true. "On earth do you have a form of entertainment that broadcast into electronic devices in your home?"

"You mean television." Her face scrunched up into a puzzled expression.

"That may be what you call it." He nodded. "You don't have one in this house. I think you may be on what we call a reality program."

"Are you kidding me? Reality TV?"

He hushed her, cautioning her to keep her voice down. "I have a device in my pocket. We can check."

He pulled out a gadget smaller than a cell phone and clicked on something on the bottom. Suddenly a 3D image immerged like a hologram in front of her. It was her and Cody and Nick in the kitchen.

"No. No," she yelled. "Not a reality TV show."

* * *

Nick kept jostling her shoulder, or was that Cody? Why didn't they stop? Kristy opened her eyes. A man's face loomed but a breath span away, totally human, though large and square, featuring a kind smile and dark eyes. From his wrinkles and the patch of gray on his balding head, she guessed his age at mid-sixties. He had sun-baked brown skin, rather than blue. She'd never seen him before, yet there was something vaguely familiar about his face. He nudged her to wake up.

"Good morning," the man greeted her in a booming voice.

Startled, she jerked her head off the steering wheel. "I must have dozed off." She glanced at the blue sky. No green hue, no double moon. "Cody." She whipped her head toward the backseat where he lay, stretched out, sleeping.

Through the grogginess of her mind, she breathed one word, "In."

With a twinge of disappointment and relief, Kristy realized it must have been a dream. She'd awakened when it started to become a nightmare as she realized she was part of a reality TV show.

She swerved back to the man. "What happened?"

He let out a hardy laugh. "It looks like you ran out of gas. Your gauge is on empty."

"I remember that." Kristy's voice held a hoarse, frog-like sound from sleep, she cleared her throat.

"I've got a gas can in my trunk. That'll give you two gallons to get you back to town." He sauntered over to his faded-red sedan.

"Thank you." She stepped out her the car and blinked her eyes to clear the daze of the dream. It had seemed so real. As she yanked on the handle of the back door, Cody opened his eyes.

"Mommy, where are we?" He clutched his sword.

"On the highway where we saw the lights." She glanced over at the white-haired, Good Samaritan as he pulled a red jug with a long sprout out of his trunk and walked over to her car.

"Oh, did you see them?" He poured the contents of the gas can into her tank.

"Yes, I did." Cody leapt out of the car with sword in hand. "Mommy and I went to In. Blue people with square heads live there."

"What?" Kristy squatted down, eye level with Cody. "Did you dream that too?"

"No, Mommy. It wasn't a dream. I pinched you, remember."

"Kids say the darndest things." The old man winked as he pulled the long spout out of her tank. "You'll be able to get back to Marfa now, but you'll have to put in more gas to go anywhere else."

Still baffled, she stood and turned to the man. "Thank you. We drove into town last night and I forgot to check the gauge. I was so excited about seeing the lights." She didn't know him well enough to come clean about her money problems.

"It happens a lot around here. You know, since you're sightseeing and what not, you should check out our courthouse. It's quite a sight." He stowed the empty can in the trunk. "Go ahead and start it up."

She sat at the wheel and turned the key. The engine purred. "I don't know what I would have done without you."

"Yes ma'am." He opened his car door and sat at the wheel. "By the way my name is Joe Azat, call me Joe. If you need anything just ask for me." He waved as he drove off.

Cody climbed into the back seat. "Mommy, he looks like the blue man, who showed us to the lady, who gave us necklaces with blue rocks." He grabbed his neck. "Where is it?"

"Gone. We're back on earth now." Images of In spun through her mind. "You're right, Cody, Mr. Azat does look like Yog, just less blue with a rounder, smaller head." She raked her teeth against her upper lip. "This is so weird. You know, they both wanted us to go to a government office."

As she drove into Marfa, Kristy reflected on the lights and her visit to the land of In. "You know, Cody, there we had our lucky turquoise, but I've always believed you make your own luck in life, and I have a better idea of how to do that now."

"How Mommy?" He whacked the plastic blade against the car seat.

"In the dream, I had confidence. I didn't think, 'I'm not good enough to live in a mansion or to have a good job.' Instead, I felt important. Usually, I act as if I don't matter at all. So Cody, I'm going to change the way I think about myself."

She turned off Highway 90 onto Highland Street. "Another thing is I took advice from strangers. They weren't even human, but I let them help me. I usually try to do everything by myself."

She pulled into the parking lot of the elegant peach-toned county courthouse and gazed up at the shiny, gray dome where a statue of the goddess of justice stood, watching over Marfa.

"I'm going to try the changes I made in my dream and see how they work for me here." As Cody unbuckled his seat belt, Kristy stepped out of the car. "Come on, punkin."

They scampered up the steps and inside, holding hands. She sauntered to the first counter.

Kristy tried to remember what she'd said to the blue woman. "I'm new here and I need a job and a place to say."

"Wrong office, hun." The lady behind the counter pointed to her left. "Down the hall and take a right. That'll bring you to Mr. Fife's office. He's the one interviewing for the file clerk position."

"I have a lot of experience as a file clerk." Kristy knew she was on the right track. "Thank you." She grabbed Cody's hand and as soon as she entered Mr. Fife's office, her breath stopped. "Nick."

Her gaze devoured his thick crop of black hair and the muscles rippling beneath the teal fabric of his polo shirt.

"Yes, do I know you?" From behind a desk cluttered with paper and manila file folders, he stood to his full height "How did you know my name?"

Shocked at seeing him, Kristy took a deep breath to get her bearings. "No, no you just look like someone I knew once, his name was Nick, too."

Nick shifted his brawny shoulders into a shrug. "It's a common name. Are you here for the job?" His blue gaze swept over her and then he flashed a smile at Cody.

"Yes. I worked as file clerk for two years for an insurance company in San Antonio."

"Sounds perfect. Go ahead and fill this out."

She took the application from him and as she sat, Cody plopped down in a chair beside her. She wrote as fast as she could and handed the paperwork back to Nick. She knew she msut be blushing. She kept staring at his lips. She felt hot and had to battle this yearning to press her lips against his. Just as she had on In.

Now seated in the captain-style chair at his desk, he glanced over her application. "So how did you hear about the job?" Nick leaned back.

"Mr. Azat . . . Joe . . . told me I should stop by."

"If Joe recommended you, that's good enough for me. You do need to pass a drug test and background check, if that won't be a problem, you have the job." He laid the application on his desk. "Can you start tomorrow? I know it's short notice."

"Tomorrow is great."

"Good." Nick leaned forward. "I've had some trouble finding people because of the hours, but since I see him," he nodded at Cody, "I know it's perfect for you. It's part time. 8:00 – 3:00 so you can put him on the bus in the morning and be home when he gets back from school."

"No babysitters," She said aloud.

"Mom, that's like In." Cody's brown eyes gleamed.

"That is if you live close by. Where are you staying?"

Kristy's gaze rested on Nick's questioning eyes. "Good question." It reminded her she'd be sleeping in the car for a while. "I'm new in town and I haven't settled in a place yet."

"Really?" His brows arched. "This may be out of hand, but since my mother's death, I've moved out of the garage apartment and into the main house." Nick leaned forward. "I really need to rent the place. I can take an early break and show it to you. It's a ten-minute walk from here."

"Please." A bubbly sensation surged through her.

All three of them stood at the same time. Nick held the office door open for her and Cody. From the back of the courthouse, they strolled down the street to a red brick home. He led her across the yard, behind that house, to the white, wooden garage apartment.

"It comes furnished." Nick unlocked the door and showed her through the parlor to the first bedroom.

Against the sidewall stood a twin bed draped with a colorful quilt, although Kristy could only see half of it. The end of the bed was cluttered with open boxes, brimming with toys. She spotted He-man, Mutant Ninja Turtles, and Transformer figures. In the middle of the floor lay an old Nintendo system with a stack of games beside it. A stuffed Count Dracula and Kermit the frog rested on a white rocking chair in the corner. A basketball and a baseball bat stuck out of a large open box, shoved against the back window. Next to it, a lava lamp and a plastic sword topped a tall wooden dresser.

"Oh, yeah, I haven't finished cleaning the place. My mom never threw out my old toys. You're welcome to them."

"Yes, I want them," Cody piped.

Kristy jumped aside as her son dashed by her and into his bedroom. He pulled the transformers out of the box.

"I haven't cleaned out the fridge or the pantry either. You'll find some pots, pans, silverware, and plenty of canned food. They might come in handy. Since you're starting work tomorrow, I know you won't have time to shop."

"Thank you." Kristy pinched herself to make sure she wasn't dreaming.

"I don't know if I mentioned it, but the first months' rent is free and no deposit is needed, since we're working together. The background check for the job will more than clear you to rent. So I don't need to run a credit check." Nick's mouth quirked with humor. "After all, I know where you work and how much you make."

Kristy giggled softly at his banter. She schooled her emotions, and asked the all-important probing question. "Are you sure your wife doesn't want to meet me first?" She held her breath, waiting for his response.

He shook his head. "Oh, I'm not married."

"I'll take it." She tried to steady her racing heart. "I know Cody and I will love Marfa."

Cody darted out of his new bedroom and ran up to Nick. "Do you eat blue worms?"

He rolled his vibrant eyes at Kristy. "Is my tongue blue, something like that?"

"No, he has blue worms on his brain."

"Are you sure?" Nick's brows arched. "How did he know?"

Kristy shrugged. "Know what?"

"It's my only vice. I've loved them since I was a kid." Nick dug into his pocket and retrieved a plastic baggy full of gummy worms. "I only like the blue ones." He held the bag out to Cody. "Have one."

"Thank you." Cody stuck one end of a candy worm in his mouth.

Half a blue gummy worm dangled between Cody's lips, as he made a yummm, yummm, yummm sound.

Kristy and Nick burst into full-hearted laugher together.

Nick took a deep breath. He felt so happy around this woman and her son. He'd just met her but he felt like he knew her. He kind of did though it made no sense. She looked so much like the woman in his dream last night. He'd had another dream of those blue people but this was the weirdest, he was on a reality TV show on another planet. He'd need to stop watching TV late at night.

The way she kept looking at his lips was driving him crazy though he probably imagined it. Still she'd even licked her full lips as her eyes held a glint of desire. Maybe that was just what he wanted to see. She stood so close to him, he could feel the heat of her body. He wanted to reach out and grab her and suddenly she was standing right next to him, leaning her head up to his. His breath caught in his throat. Nick's heart hammered.

He knew it was inappropriate. He would be this woman's boss and her landlord but she gazed at him with a wide eyed, dreamy look in her eyes.

Silently, their eyeys melted into each other's as they found themselves lost in each other's gaze. Their lips slowly drew closer. He merely brushed his lips across hers but his mouth burned from the touch. A shiver of heat coursed through his body. His nerve endings tingled. The muscles in his lower abdomen drew tight with need.

He caught himself just in time before he grabbed her and crushed his mouth against hers as he longed to. "I'm so sorry. I didn't meant to—"

"No." Kristy cut him off. "I think it was I who kissed you."

"Really." He cleared his throat, now muted with lust. So he hadn't imagined it. She liked him. "This is your fist night. You have too much to do to cook or anything . You should celebrate your new job and your new place." He flashed what he hoped was his most devastating smile. "Let me take you and Cody out to dinner."

"I'd like that. Thank you." "I'll pick you up around 8 pm. I'll take you to Jett's Grill. It's in the El Paisano hotel." He shrugged. "It's named after James Dean's character in Giant."

"I know." Her entire face beamed as she smiled. "I'd love to go."

"So at eight then." He placed one hand of each of her shoulders. "Welcome to Marfa." He hugged her to him, breathing in her soft, flora scent.

When he released her, she cocked her head and met his gaze. A throbbing warmth filled him.

"Thank you," Kristy said. "I think I'll like it here in Marfa." She pressed her lips together as if in thought. "I'm not sure about the lights though."

"Yeah, I should warn you about them. I had a strange encounter with one several weeks ago."

"Did it seem to watch you? She rubbed her teeth against her lip. "Chase you?"

"You too?"

"Why would a light watch us." Her brows arched

"A light or something that controls the light." He shook his head. "I don't know. Something about us must interest them."

She let out a giggle. "It's so silly. Lights chasing us. I must have just been tired and half imagined it. Probably just stressed about running out of gas on the road at night like that. "

"Could be. The lights are strange though and no one knows what causes them."

At that moment, he saw a flash, a small wink of a light by the mirror on the wall. It reminded him of a camera for some reason. He blinked his eyes but it was gone. *I must be imagining things also*, he thought. Nick fixed his gaze back on her. "It did bother me though. In fact, I had bad dreams ever since it chased me, until last night." He smiled at Kristy but he didn't want to tell her he'd dreamed about her and scare her off.

"Really?"

Something about the glint in her eyes made him suspect that she already knew. "Yes. Very interesting dreams. One day I'll tell you about them

ALSO BY CORNELIA AMIRI

Other books by Cornelia Amiri who also writes as Maeve Alpin:

Druids In The Mist

The Warrior and the Druidess

Prince Of Powys

Moon Goddess Wife

Timeless Voyage

The Celtic Fox

The Celtic Vixen

The Scottish Selkie

Queen Of Kings

Back To The One I Love

Peace Love Music

A Fine Cauldron Of Fish

The Wolf And The Druidess

The Dragon And the Druidess

Pendragon's Obsession

To Love A London Ghost

The Ghost Lights of Marfa

Starry Conquest

As Timeless As Stone

As Timeless As Magic

The Brass Octopus

A Woman of Intellectual Means

Code of Misconduct

I Love You More

Reach

Need Fire - box set

Swords and Roses - Bundle

Warrior Hearts – Bundle

Scandalously Yours – Box Set

Mother's Day Magic – Box Set

Portals Volume Three – Box Set

Portals Volume Six – Box Set

Sneak Peek Samplers: Historical Romance –Box Set

Sneak Peek Samplers: Fantasy Romance – Box set

ABOUT THE AUTHOR

Cornelia Amiri, who also writes as Maeve Alpin, is the author of 31 published books. Known as the Celtic Romance Queen, she writes Celtic Fantasy Romance, Celtic Historical Romance, Steampunk Romance and Sci-fi Romance. She lives in Houston Texas as does her son and granddaughter and her cat, Severus. Severus is a writer's cat, he loves books. He likes to knock them off the bookshelf, sit on them, and sniff the open pages. He also uses the computer, he sits on it, lays on top of it, and walks across the keyboard. Cornelia is working on a soon to be released Celtic Fantasy Romance, <u>The Dragon and the Druidess</u>, the second novella in the Druidry and the Beast series.

SIGN UP FOR MY NEWSLETTER

Please sign up for my Newsletter to get the latest information on my new releases and my free book releases here.

Get your eBook autographed here.

Please visit my website, my facebook page, my twitter and my pinterest.

I Love You More published by Author, Cornelia Amiri

Copyright @2016

All rights held by author. The reproduction or other use of any part of this publication without the prior written consent of the rights holder is an infringement of the copyright law

www.ingramcontent.com/pod-product-compliance
Lightning Source LLC
Chambersburg PA
CBHW051801130726
47987CB00003B/1061